FOURTH OF JULY BEAR

KATHRYN LASKY

ILLUSTRATED BY

HELEN COGANCHERRY

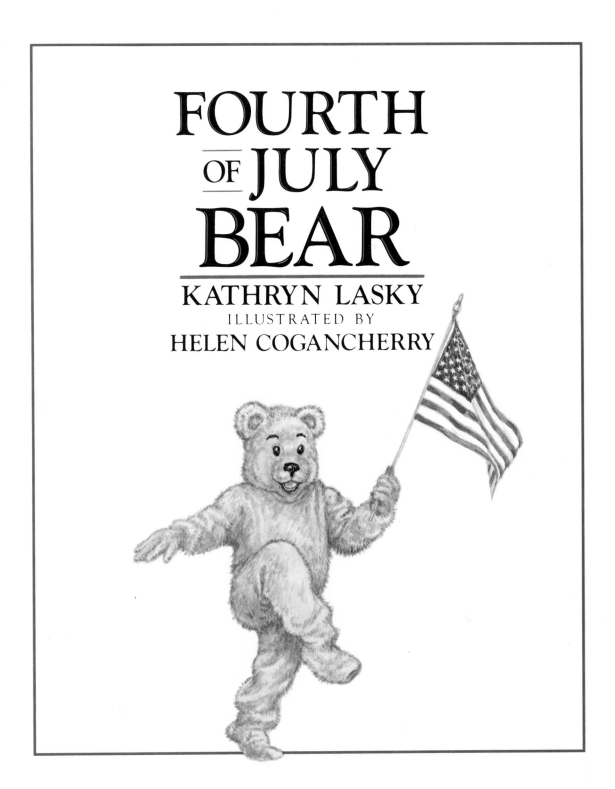

MORROW JUNIOR BOOKS / NEW YORK

E
LAS

Library of Congress Cataloging-in-Publication Data
Lasky, Kathryn.
Fourth of July bear / Kathryn Lasky : illustrated by Helen Cogancherry.
p.   cm.
Summary: Spending summer vacation on a Maine island, Rebecca
misses her best friend Emily until she meets Amanda, who invites
Rebecca to be in the Fourth of July parade.
ISBN 0-688-08287-4 (trade).—ISBN 0-688-08288-2 (library)
[1. Friendship—Fiction. 2. Parades—Fiction. 3. Fourth of July—
Fiction. 4. Islands—Fiction.] I. Cogancherry, Helen, ill.
II. Title.   III. Title: 4th of July bear.
PZ7.L3274Fo   1991
[E]—dc20   90-37422   CIP   AC

This is Meribah's book
K.L.
To my husband, Herb, with love
H.C.

There is an island waiting for me, in a bay in Maine. My mom says it's shaped like a dolphin swimming in the sea, and we can reach it only by a long, slender bridge. I live in the city. They finally fixed our sidewalk so it is perfect for roller skating. The new pavement is smooth as frosting all the way down to Church Street. My best friend, Emily, will get to skate here all summer. I won't.

The bridge to the island rumbles when we drive across it. There is water all around us. On the other side of the bridge there is a tar road, and then the tar turns into dirt.

"This is where our house will be," says my mom. She is holding a map in the front seat of the car and turns around to show me. "You see?" She points her finger to a piece of land that juts out from the island. "It looks like the tail of a dolphin. And our house is where an edge of the tail meets the edge of the sea."

"I'm not sure if I want to live on the tail of any island," I say.

"I heard there is a little girl who lives there, too."

"She's probably older."

"No, I don't think so," my mom says.

But I know that even if she is exactly my age and born in the same month on the same day and in the same exact minute as me, she won't be as nice as Emily.

The tail of the island is called a point. And the point where the house is has trees as tall as castle tops. The house has gray shingles and white roses scrambling up the sides. My bed is small and the ceiling slants. When I go to sleep that night, I miss my room in the city. I am sleeping on the tail of a dolphin and my real home seems far away.

"The strawberries come first," the lady says. Her name is May and she lives down the road. "Then the blackberries, the raspberries, and finally the blueberries!"

It is blackberry time now, and we go picking in the field on the other side of the point. Another girl is there with her mother. I stay close to my mom and sometimes peek at her through the tall grass or from behind my mom's skirt.

Picking berries is better than swimming. The water is so cold that after you get out, you shiver for a long time. But then my dad found a place where the water is warmed by the rocks when the tide is high. One day I swam out to a beautiful rock with a notch just the right size for my hand. I call it a catching spot. You can hold on and rest and catch your breath before swimming back to shore. But still, swimming in the rock pool is not as much fun as skating with Emily.

We see the little girl from the blackberry field at the post office when we go to get our mail. Her name is Amanda. She is my age, but I am taller. Our mothers say how nice it would be if we played together. But we both look down at the wooden floor of the post office and curl our toes. She has some pink polish on her big toenail.

Then one day there is a scratching at our screen door.

"Would you like to be a bear?" Amanda asks through the screen.

"A what?"

"A bear," she says again. "A Fourth of July Bear and ride in the parade on Fire Engine Number One. My mother told me to ask you."

"What do they do in a Fourth of July parade?" I ask. "I've never seen one." I whisper that part down my shirt.

"People build floats on flatbeds. You know, kind of like floors with wheels, and you hook them onto trucks. Last year we had an old-fashioned schoolhouse float, and I was a schoolgirl with a bonnet and slate! And one year they wanted the Statue of Liberty, so my cousin Mary was covered with silver makeup, and she wore a crown and carried a torch."

Amanda giggles. "Mary had to hold up the torch from the fire station all the way round the bend to Beck's store and then back again. Her arm got real tired!"

I thought a minute about her cousin, all silver, riding on a float with her arm in the air.

"So do you want to be a bear with me?" she asks again. "You don't have to hold anything. Just growl." She giggles a little more.

"Maybe." I don't look at her.

"See you later," she says through the screen door.

My dad has come up behind me. "That sounds like fun, Becca. Becca Bear!"

"Oh, Daddy!"

I just wish Emily could be the other bear. But I don't say so. I only think it.

The next morning my mom and I are at the post office when May, the berry lady, comes up and says, "I hear you're going to be a bear."

"Maybe..." I just start to say the word and already she is pulling something out of her pocket. It's a tape measure. "I am the chief bear-suit maker on the island," she says. She measures me right there in front of the post office, writing down the numbers on a little piece of paper:

neck to ankle:	38 inches
shoulder to wrist:	16 inches
width across back:	11 inches
width around head:	21 inches

When she is finished she says, "I have to go and catch me one more bear."

Three times in one week I go to May's house so she can fit the costume. Amanda is always there, too. We stand as still as we can in the kitchen while May pins and cuts and tucks and trims.

"You girls can talk while I'm doing this," May tells us. But we don't say anything to each other.

Each time she finishes, May gives us both a cookie. We eat them slowly as we walk back to the point, hoping to make the cookies last until we get home. Amanda has to eat even more slowly than I do because she lives farther away.

"Do you ever go roller skating?" I ask one day.

"No."

"I do. At home we have the greatest sidewalk in the whole world for roller skating. My best friend Emily and I roller-skate all the time."

Amanda just says, "Oh," and looks out at the ocean. Maybe she is trying to imagine a sidewalk there.

By the third of July, our costumes are finished. They are made of fake fur with invisible slits to keep us cool. There is stuffing sewn into the front to give us poochy tummies, and the heads have big black glass bear eyes. We try the costumes on in May's kitchen.

"Is the fire engine high?" I ask.

"Not too high," Amanda says. "Here, have a cookie." She feeds me through the little bear mouth.

"I might be a little bit scared," I admit. "I've never been in a parade before. And I've never ridden on top of a fire engine, either."

"It's fun, and there are ladders on both sides. You can't fall off."

May finally says, "Okay, bears, you're ready! Be sure to wear your bathing suits underneath so you won't get too hot tomorrow."

But the next day isn't very hot at all. The wind blows off the ocean, bringing fog. There is fog in our fur and mist in our whiskers. The fire engine looks gigantic.

"This fog will burn off," Fire Chief Haskell says. First he lifts me up onto the engine and then Amanda. "Here are your cubs, Smokey." Smokey is Mr. Eaton, and he seems as tall as a tree in his Smokey Bear costume. He stands between us, and we each grip a ladder with our paws.

Fire Engine Number One is third in the parade. Just in front is a bunch of kids dressed up like firecrackers. They are wearing painted cardboard boxes and have pinwheels and pipe cleaners and tinfoil whirligig thingamajigs sticking out of their hair.

The whistle blows, the band starts to play, and the parade begins to move down the hill toward the harbor. Amanda gives a little growl, and then so do I. She waves, and so do I. I can tell she's good at this.

There are at least a hundred people on both sides of the street. They cheer, and in the harbor, boats toot their horns.

The parade goes past the fire station and then the school. By the time it gets to the post office, Amanda and I are really good at waving with our paws. Our moms and dads walk alongside the fire engine for a while—until we growl them away.

May is standing at the big bend in the road, and right through the tuba's boom we growl, "May!"

We growl at Pete Hardy, the carpenter who fixed our back door, and at Bobby Williams, the lobster fisherman.

And when the parade crosses the causeway over the millpond, we get a good look at the very front of the parade, where the Grand Marshal and his wife ride in a car with the top down. Mrs. Grand Marshal is very large. She wears a dress covered with hundreds of daisies. Amanda says she looks like Prouty Point—a place near the dolphin's head that blows all July with daisies and, in August, with Queen Anne's lace.

Chief Haskell is right. The fog does burn off, and by the time the parade is finished, it is hot. My dad buys us ice cream cones and I drip a little on my fur. I am so hot and sticky I can't think of anything except swimming. I remember the rock pool and the catching spot.

"Do bears swim?" I ask Amanda.

"They must."

"Let's get our parents to take us to the rock pool."

At the beach we step out of our bear costumes, fold them carefully, and put them on a rock way above the high-tide line so they will stay dry.

"Want to know how I always jump into the water?" I say to Amanda.

"How?"

"Watch!"

"One, two, three . . . Rebecca Grace Albright!" And I fly off the rock. I'm not a bear anymore. I'm me. And then Amanda does the same.

The cold water slides over our skin. I am so glad that I don't have fur so I can feel the sea and the waves, and that my eyes are real and not glass bear eyes. I open them underwater and see the spotted round rocks that look like jewels. I see Amanda's legs and the polka dots of her bathing suit. We swim to the big rock, and I show Amanda the catching spot. It fits her hand, too. We pull ourselves up on top of the rock, which is crusty with barnacles. My knee gets scraped and the salt stings. Amanda scrapes her knee, too. We lick our knees and growl and wave to our moms on the beach.

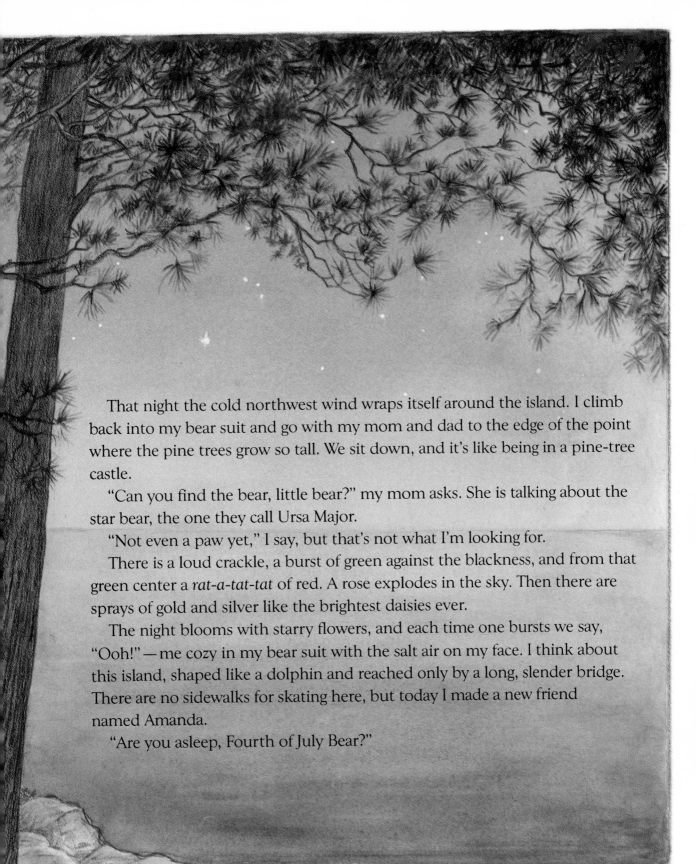

That night the cold northwest wind wraps itself around the island. I climb back into my bear suit and go with my mom and dad to the edge of the point where the pine trees grow so tall. We sit down, and it's like being in a pine-tree castle.

"Can you find the bear, little bear?" my mom asks. She is talking about the star bear, the one they call Ursa Major.

"Not even a paw yet," I say, but that's not what I'm looking for.

There is a loud crackle, a burst of green against the blackness, and from that green center a *rat-a-tat-tat* of red. A rose explodes in the sky. Then there are sprays of gold and silver like the brightest daisies ever.

The night blooms with starry flowers, and each time one bursts we say, "Ooh!" — me cozy in my bear suit with the salt air on my face. I think about this island, shaped like a dolphin and reached only by a long, slender bridge. There are no sidewalks for skating here, but today I made a new friend named Amanda.

"Are you asleep, Fourth of July Bear?"

I pretend to be asleep for just a second, and then I laugh and jump up. "One, two, three ... Fourth of July Bear!" I shout.

And as the sky explodes with roses, I dance a firecracker dance on the dolphin's tail.